MOTHS & MOTHERS, FEATHERS & FATHERS

A Story About a Tiny Owl Named Squib

Written and Illustrated by
Larry Shles

Houghton Mifflin Company Boston 1984

Library of Congress Cataloging in Publication Data

Shles, Lawrence M.
Moths & mothers, feathers & fathers.

Previously published as: Moths & fathers, feathers &
mothers. 1st ed. 1983.
Summary: Although he is a tiny owl that cannot hoot or
fly, Squib's curiosity leads him into adventures that
sometimes inspire frightening emotions that he must
learn to identify and express.
1. Children's stories, American. [1. Emotions—Fic-
tion. 2. Owls—Fiction] I. Title. II. Title: Moths
and mothers, feathers and fathers.
PZ7.S5585Mo   1984   [E]   84-10846
ISBN 0-395-36695-X
ISBN 0-395-36555-4 (pbk.)

Printed in the United States of America

Cloth   P   Pbk.   AL   10 9 8 7 6 5 4 3 2 1

TO
MY PARENTS,
WHO PLANTED
THE FEELING,

ILENE,
WHO PROVIDED
THE FAITH,

PAT,
WHO INSPIRED
THE FORM,

AND
SPECIAL
THANKS TO
GEORGE NICKS,
WHOSE SENSITIVITY
AND CRITICAL EYE
HELPED INFUSE THIS
WORK WITH ADDITIONAL
DRAMA AND COHESION.

Squib was an unusually tiny owl who couldn'

hoot or fly.

Longing to see the world, he would perch
on the feelers of moths and soar over valleys
of brilliant color, rivers of refreshing spray
and mountains echoing with melodious song.

On his journeys he rarely thought of home or
his parents. He was too busy exploring.
Then, unexpectedly…

something would startle Squib and...

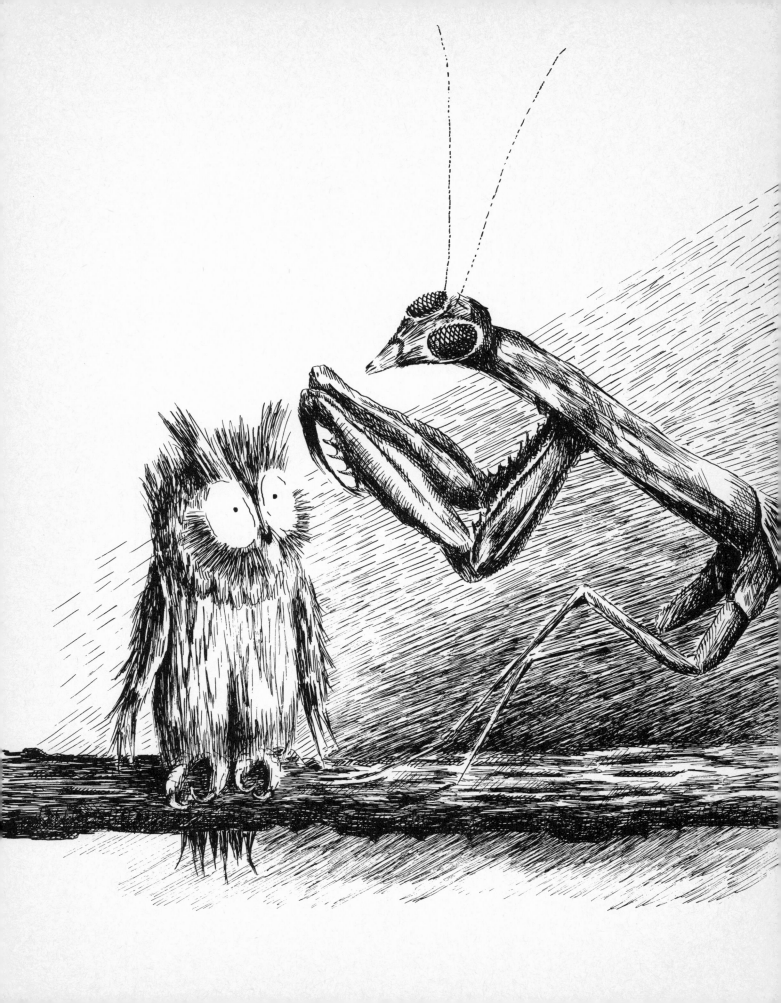

he'd rush back to the warmth and softness of his mother and father. He'd snuggle down in their softest feathers, hiding from the rest of the world. There his feelings were warm and calm, like a toy boat bobbing ever so slightly on a still lake.

He had no idea that those feelings had a name.

Squib would always venture out again.
Occasionally, though, he surprised himself
and journeyed much too far. Just one more
step, he would say…and then another, and
another, and then suddenly…

he would find himself alone and lost. He would hide behind the thorns, almost unable to move, praying for his mother or father to find him.

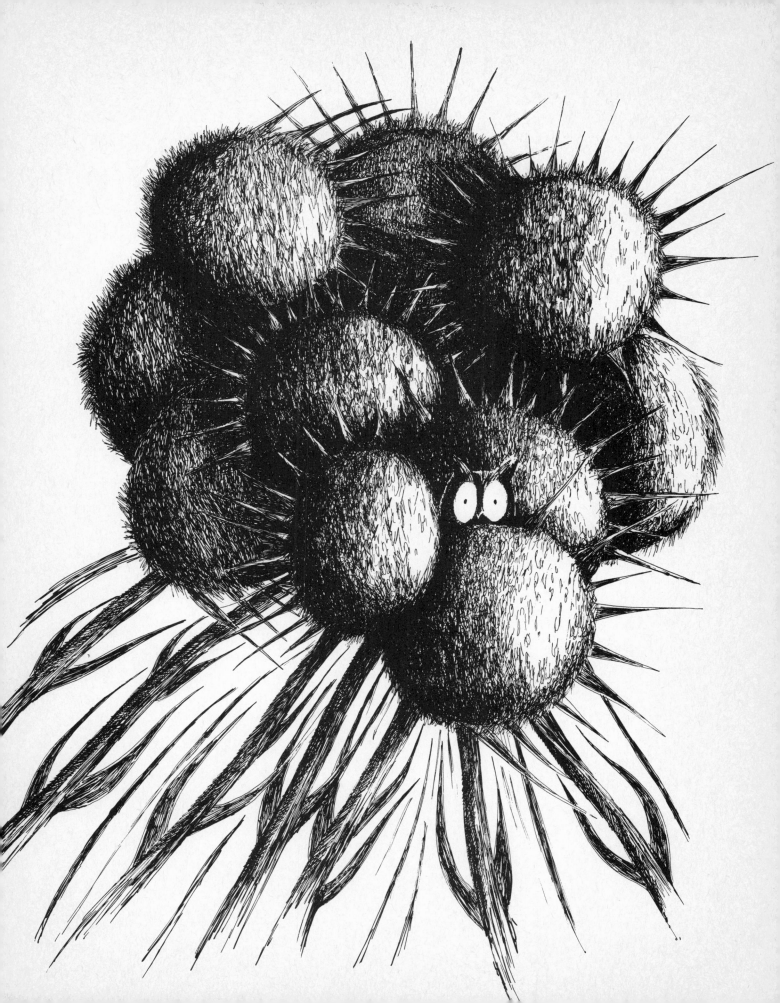

His prayers were always answered. When h[e]
tremble a little, remember his ordeal, promis[e]

was back and safe in their down, Squib would
himself never to go too far again, and, with a sigh…

fall asleep and dream dreams of moths and father

and feathers and mothers.

The times when Squib went out with his parents were wonderful. His father would hold him high on a tuft so that he could see the puppet show at the fair. Squib could feel his father's strength and see how unbelievably tall he was. Squib would feel strong and tall himself.

He didn't yet know that those feelings had a name.

And while perched on his mother's foot as she danced through the meadow, a free, airy feeling welled up inside Squib. How much fun it was, he thought, to swirl around without having to lift his own feet.

Then, tired from the excitement of the day, Squib would look forward to bedtime…well, that part of bedtime just before sleeptime. His parents would tuck him into soft down and tell him a story in the most velvety, soothing hoots you can imagine. Lying there listening, feeling the up and down breathing, smelling the special smells of his mother and father, Squib felt complete.

Did that feeling have a name?

Squib and his father loved playing games together. One of their favorites was catch. Squib would giggle and gasp with joy as he was tossed from tuft to tuft.

And when his father purposely fumbled him, Squib would plummet downward, landing softly in delicate feathers that would close in around him, wrapping him in a feeling of contentment.

When noisy storms rumbled in, Squib's father would hover over him, sheltering him under a huge wing. The crash of thunder would explode in his ears. The rain would gush off the wing. The cool wind would creep into his shelter. Yet Squib would feel safe and tucked away.

And that feeling has a name.

Squib never really looked forward to being sick, but when he caught cold, he could sense the extra concern of his mother and father. They would check on him often, asking how he was feeling and if he wanted something to eat or drink. At times like these, Squib knew that their warmth and tenderness would always be there to protect him.

One day, as Squib was wandering in the heat of the afternoon sun, he came upon other young owls playing a game of roly-poly. They were clinging tightly to one another, rolling around in the dust, and hooting and hollering with great excitement.

Squib always wanted to join in any game. "Car

I play too?" Squib tooted softly.

The young owls began laughing at Squib and teasing him about his size and the ridiculous way he tooted rather than hooted. They told him they had never seen a punier, dumber looking owl, and they were going to beat him up and pull out his tail feathers.

Suddenly a dark shadow moved across him. He turned to see what had blotted out the sun. It was his mother. Her shadow had cooled the air and frightened the other owls away. Squib was overjoyed. He asked to be picked up so he could talk to his mother face to face. Tears of gratitude were in his eyes.

The desire to know what this feeling was overwhelmed him.

He looked at his mother. He wanted so much to tell her what he was feeling and was searching for the words…when he noticed something he had never seen before. He could see <u>his</u> reflection in her eyes. His expression was the same as hers. She must be feeling what he was feeling!

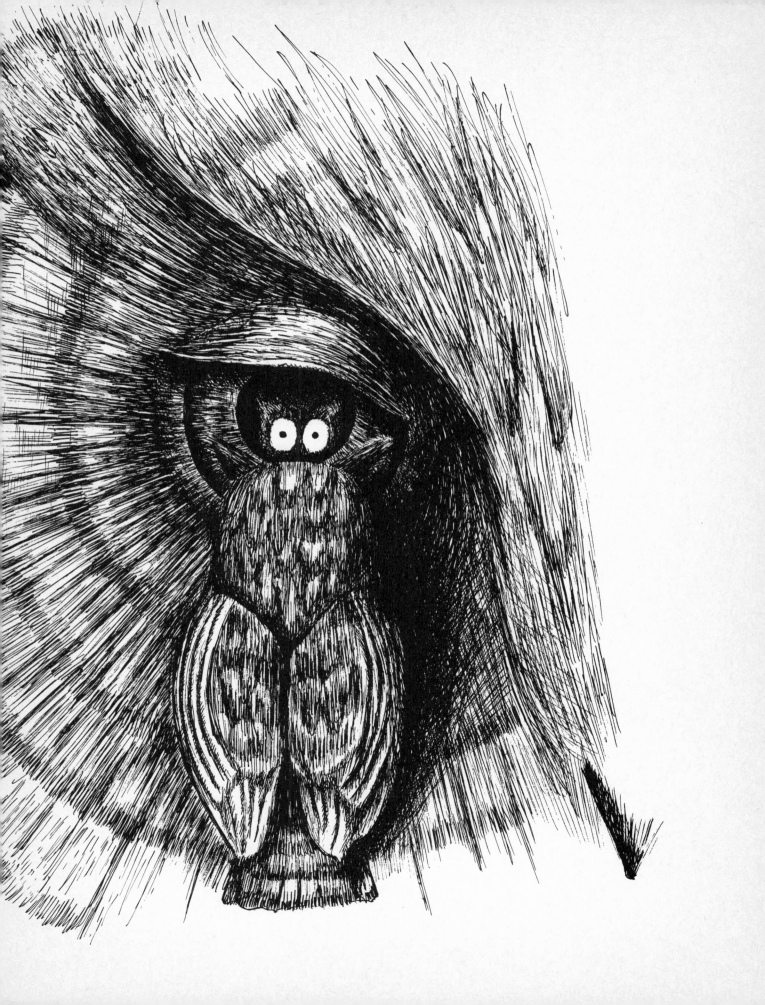

Looking into his mother's eyes
was like looking into a sunrise!

At last he could give words to what he was feeling. As sweetly and softly as he could, in a purring toot that was as close to a hoot as he could come, Squib whispered,

"I love you."

To be continued...